RAGGEDY GRANNY
STORIES

RAGGEDY GRANNY
STORIES

by

Doris Thorner Salzberg

Illustrated by

Johnny, Worth and Justin Gruelle, and others

THE BOBBS-MERRILL COMPANY, INC.
Indianapolis   New York

*Raggedy Ann and Raggedy Andy and all related characters
appearing in this book are trademarks of
The Bobbs-Merrill Company, Inc.*

Cover by John Hopper

Design and production by Sally Lifland

Manufactured in the United States of America

Library of Congress Cataloging in Publication Data

Salzberg, Doris Thorner.
    Raggedy Granny stories.

    SUMMARY: Raggedy Ann, Andy, and Granny save Mr. Lollipop Tree in the
Magic Forest and meet up with the Whiznees in their own vegetable garden.
    [1. Dolls—Fiction. 2. Fantasy] I. Gruelle,
John B., 1880?-1938. II. Title.
PZ8.9.S15Rag   [Fic]   77-6113
ISBN 0-672-52354-X

ACKNOWLEDGMENTS

Special thanks to

Alice Cohan, Director, Manhasset—Great Neck Head Start Program,

Dr. Arthur Young, Director, Psychological Services of North Shore Hospital,

Dr. Daniel Salzberg, Westchester Conservation Council, Cortlandt Conservation Association, and Federation of Conservationists of Westchester County,

Paul Bather, Director, Manhasset—Great Neck Equal Opportunity Council.

RAGGEDY GRANNY AND THE WHIZNEES

"What a lovely vegetable garden!" said Raggedy Granny, pleased to see the neat rows Raggedy Ann and Raggedy Andy were planting.

"Your bow tie is all lit up," called Raggedy Andy, looking up from the new spring garden he was digging. He knew that when Raggedy Granny was happy her bow tie lit up.

"Please pass the watermelon seeds," said Raggedy Ann, looking up from the straight rows of freshly turned earth.

"Can you wait until I finish planting this row of corn?" Raggedy Andy called over his shoulder.

There was a big patch of mud on Raggedy Ann's cheek, which made her big smile look bigger.

Raggedy Andy was covered with mud from head to toe.

And then

it

happened.

9

The ground shook,

seeds went flying,

the neat rows of earth toppled.

"It's the Whiznees! They're whizzing through the woods again. They mess up everything in sight," groaned Raggedy Andy.

They whizzed by so fast, the dirt and dead leaves swirled up in a cloud. Squirrels scooted up trees, woodchucks chucked into the ground, chipmunks raced by, and the rabbits' bushy tails bobbed up and down as they ran to hide themselves. Bushes and plants parted to let them pass through.

The biggest Whiznee whizzed close to Raggedy Ann and Raggedy Andy.

Raggedy Ann was knocked into a tree.

Raggedy Andy fell into a bramble bush.

First Raggedy Granny pulled Raggedy Ann down from the tree. Then she hurried over to Raggedy Andy, who was struggling to free himself from the bramble bush.

"Give me your hand, Andy," said Raggedy Granny, reaching down and pulling him from under the branches. "This nonsense has to stop. We can't have those Whiznees whizzing through here every spring upsetting everyone and everything in the forest."

When the cloud had settled, all the Whiznees were gone except the oldest one. His tusk was stuck so deep into the big oak tree that he couldn't pull it out no matter how hard he tried.

He pulled and he pulled and he pulled. His pink face turned purple with fear.

"Let him stay," said Raggedy Andy crossly, looking down at his torn clothing. He was angry that the Whiznees had upset his planting and ruined his garden.

"You're right—I shouldn't help him. Those Whiznees cause so much trouble. Oh, well, I guess we can't leave him there." Raggedy Granny took a magic rope out of her pocket.

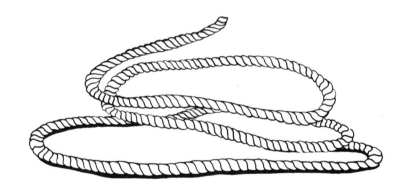

It got

bigger

and

bigger

and

bigger

When it was long enough, they wrapped it around the Whiznee's middle, and then they all pulled as hard as they could. They pulled so hard they fell over backwards, arms, legs and Whiznee all tangled up.

"Oh, my, will I ever see my Whiznee family again?" moaned the Whiznee. Raggedy Granny helped Raggedy Ann and Raggedy Andy to their feet.

The Whiznee sat there with his eyes closed tight.

"Oh, dear, the Whiznee's tusk is bent," said Raggedy Ann. "Well, we'll straighten that out as soon as we clean him up a bit."

Raggedy Granny lifted one corner of her big apron and gently cleaned the Whiznee's bent tusk. One eye opened and stared at Raggedy Granny's glasses sparkling in the sun.

Then the other eye opened.

The Whiznee seemed surprised to see Raggedy Ann's and Raggedy Andy's smiles as big as ever. Raggedy Granny was being very careful not to hurt him as she straightened his tusk.

There he was, the terrible Whiznee, sitting there with tears pouring from his big eyes and splashing over the ends of his long tusks.

"How kind you are to help me, after all the trouble we've caused," cried the Whiznee, sobbing.

"This whizzing has got to stop!" scolded Raggedy Granny. "You can't keep on causing us all this trouble. Why do you do it?"

The Whiznee wiped his eyes, wiggled his nose, and said, "Every spring, when we

come out of our cave, our wibbly knees wobble. We don't want all the animals in the woods to see us wibble wobble. They'd think we were not very strong and would take all our food. We go whizzing through the woods to frighten all the animals so they'll stay away from our cave and not touch our food."

"Oh, you foolish Whiznee," cried Raggedy Granny. "Did the animals in the woods ever, ever eat your food?"

"No," said the Whiznee.

"They are all strong and healthy, and none go hungry," Raggedy Granny went on.

"Hey, that's right," said the Whiznee.

"There's enough food for all," reminded Granny, getting up to look for her magic pot and pitcher.

By now all the animals in the woods had crept into the yard to see the terrible Whiznee sitting down with Raggedy Ann, Raggedy Andy and Raggedy Granny.

Behind them, the rest of the Whiznees were wibbling and wobbling at a distance. They had stopped their whizzing to see what was going on.

"Why don't you join us," called Raggedy Ann and Raggedy Andy.

"Please join us," called out Raggedy Granny. She was busy taking food out of her magic pot and pouring drinks from her magic pitcher.

Slowly, cautiously, the other Whiznees joined the group.

The rabbits were munching carrots. The squirrels were cracking nuts and eating them as quickly as they could. All the

animals were busy eating their favorite food and enjoying the good company.

Suddenly they realized they were all together.

The littlest Whiznee said, "I had no idea everyone would be so friendly."

"Of course," said Raggedy Granny. "The bigger the party, the better the fun."

They all danced in a circle and wibbled and wobbled and skipped and hopped until the sun went down behind the hill.

Everyone was full and everyone was tired. Some yawned, some stretched, and some sprawled on the ground to sleep.

Before the Whiznees went back to

their cave, the oldest Whiznee, who was seated in the middle of the garden, said, "I'm so ashamed of all the trouble we've caused. Raggedy Granny is right; there's surely enough food for us all."

"I'll help you replant your seeds," said the littlest Whiznee.

"We'll help you repair the bushes we trampled," said the rest of the Whiznees.

They did one more little dance, and then everyone went home.

The last thing Raggedy Ann and Raggedy Andy saw before they fell asleep was the glow of Raggedy Granny's bow tie all lit up.

RAGGEDY GRANNY'S PICNIC

Raggedy Ann's shoebutton eyes peeked out from under the covers.

The sun was shining through the playroom window—it was a beautiful summer day.

"Wake up, Raggedy Andy. Today is the day for our picnic with Raggedy Granny in the Magic Forest. Please hurry!"

Raggedy Andy loved to sleep. But today he jumped up quickly.

Raggedy Granny's picnic is in

The Magic Forest today,

The Magic Forest today,

The Magic Forest today . . .

Lu la lu la lu!

sang Raggedy Andy as he made his bed and
rushed to get ready.

28

"Ting-a-ling!" went the bell. There, standing in the doorway, was Raggedy Granny, with her big smile and her silver hair and her magic bow all aglow.

"Oh, Raggedy Granny, we're so happy to see you!" cried Raggedy Ann.

"Oh, Raggedy Granny, your bow tie is all lit up," said Raggedy Andy, giggling.

Raggedy Andy knew that when Raggedy Granny's bow tie was lit up, she was pleased.

"Oh, children, you're teasing your old grandmother again. Everyone knows bow ties don't light up," protested Raggedy Granny, with her bow tie all aglow.

"Look,

look,"

they both cried.

"Oh, nonsense! Now, now, let's get moving, or we'll miss the best time of day for our picnic."

And so they walked along the path to the Magic Forest, with their lunch pails swinging on their arms.

They walked,

and they walked,

and they walked.

The birds sang, the flowers nodded, and a noisy brook ran along.

"Raggedy Granny, help me!"

"Oh, Raggedy Andy, stop teasing Granny—you don't need help," said Raggedy Ann.

"I didn't say anything," said Raggedy Andy.

"Raggedy Granny, please help!"

"Who said that?" asked Raggedy Ann, looking around. All she could see was a large tree with orange and strawberry and cherry lollipops growing on every branch.

"I did," said the voice.

"I hear you, but I don't see you."

Copyright 1930 The Bobbs-Merrill Company, Inc.

Just then Raggedy Granny came along.

"Oh, Mr. Lollipop Tree, how good to see you. I want you to meet my grandchildren, Raggedy Ann and Raggedy Andy," said Raggedy Granny, with her bow tie all lit up.

"How do you do," said Raggedy Ann and Raggedy Andy. "We never met a lollipop tree before."

"Why, Mr. Lollipop Tree, I do believe you're crying," said Raggedy Granny.

"Oh, Raggedy Granny, I'm so glad you're here. Some folks were picnicking, and they left their fire burning. And I'm afraid all my lollipops will melt."

The three peeked around the lovely spreading lollipop tree, and there, sure enough, was a little fire, and it was growing

bigger

and

bigger

and

bigger

One of the flames reached right up to a large orange lollipop.

"Oh, how dreadful!" cried Raggedy Granny. "Hurry and get me some water from the noisy brook."

Raggedy Ann and Raggedy Andy grabbed their lunch pails. They emptied their lunches onto their picnic blanket and ran with their lunch pails to the brook.

They scooped up water and ran back as quickly as they could to put out the fire.

They splashed,

and they splashed,

and they splashed.

Still the fire spread. One flame reached out toward some low bushes.

They ran and splashed it with water.

Another flame came very close to the bushy tail of a small squirrel.

"Get that flame!" called Granny.

They ran and splashed that, too.

At last the fire was smothered.

"Oh, thank you so much. You've saved us all," said the squirrel, smiling and rubbing his bushy little tail.

The bushes were smiling too, and Mr. Lollipop Tree, with his lollipops saved, was smiling the biggest smile of all.

Raggedy Granny looked over at the tired and sopping-wet Raggedy Ann and Raggedy Andy.

"Let's have some nice hot cocoa—that will fix us up," said Raggedy Granny. She took out her magic pitcher and poured the hot sweet drink into everyone's cup.

"Thank you," said a shivering Raggedy Ann and Raggedy Andy, snuggling into the picnic blanket and sipping slowly.

Then Raggedy Granny asked them all to shake as hard as they could to help make heat for her magic pot. Everyone shook.

"Ho, ho, I can't shake very much harder," said Mr. Lollipop Tree, laughing, "or I'll lose all my lollipops."

They shook,

and they shook,

and they shook.

And when the pot was opened, there was a lovely steaming-hot lunch of chicken and potatoes and even a dumpling.

For dessert Mr. Lollipop Tree offered each of his three friends a lollipop.

"May we pick one?" asked Raggedy Ann.

"Oh, yes," said the Tree. "Picking my pops is good for me, because new ones grow in their places." And he lowered one of his biggest branches almost to the ground so that his friends could reach the juicy lollipops.

"Oh, thank you," cried Raggedy Andy and Raggedy Ann. "These are the best lollipops we've ever eaten."

Raggedy Granny's tie lit up with pleasure.

Everyone agreed that this was the best picnic they had ever had.

Each one poured himself one more drink from Raggedy Granny's magic

pitcher, and then they began to pack up for the long walk home.

"Goodbye, Mr. Lollipop Tree. So nice to know you."

"Goodbye, Mr. Lollipop Tree. I'm so glad we could help you and your friends," said Raggedy Granny.

And the family of three, happy but tired, started for home.

They walked,

and they walked,

and they walked.

Raggedy Ann and Raggedy Andy climbed into bed as soon as they got home.

"Good night, and pleasant dreams," said Raggedy Granny, kissing and hugging them lovingly.

The last thing they saw before they fell asleep was Raggedy Granny's magic bow tie all aglow.